INDEPENDENCE DAY

THE ORIGINAL MOVIE ADAPTATION

RALPH MACCHIO
PHIL CRAIN
LEONARD KIRK
ROD WHIGHAM
TERRY PALLOT

TITAN
COMICS

INDEPENDENCE DAY: THE ORIGINAL MOVIE ADAPTATION

ISBN: 9781785853357

Published by Titan Comics, a division of Titan Publishing Group, Ltd. 144 Southwark Street, London, SE1 0UP.

Contains material originally published in Independence Day #0 and Independence Day #1-2.

A CIP catalogue record for this title is available from the British Library. First edition: July 2016.

10 9 8 7 6 5 4 3 2 1

Printed in China. TC1644.

WWW.TITAN-COMICS.COM

TITAN COMICS

COLLECTION EDITOR
Nick Jones

COLLECTION SUPERVISOR
Andrew James

ASSISTANT COLLECTION EDITORS
Gabriela Houston & Jessica Burton

COLLECTION DESIGNER
Rob Farmer

SENIOR EDITOR
Steve White

TITAN COMICS EDITORIAL
Lizzie Kaye, Tom Williams

PRODUCTION ASSISTANT
Peter James

PRODUCTION SUPERVISORS
Maria Pearson, Jackie Flook

PRODUCTION MANAGER
Obi Onuora

STUDIO MANAGER
Emma Smith

SENIOR SALES MANAGER
Steve Tothill

BRAND MANAGER, MARKETING
Lucy Ripper

SENIOR MARKETING & PRESS OFFICER
Owen Johnson

DIRECT SALES & MARKETING MANAGER
Ricky Claydon

COMMERCIAL MANAGER
Michelle Fairlamb

PUBLISHING MANAGER
Darryl Tothill

PUBLISHING DIRECTOR
Chris Teather

OPERATIONS DIRECTOR
Leigh Baulch

EXECUTIVE DIRECTOR
Vivian Cheung

PUBLISHER
Nick Landau

ID4
INDEPENDENCE DAY
THE ORIGINAL MOVIE ADAPTATION

INDEPENDENCE DAY #0

Written by: Phil Crain
Based on Ideas and Concepts by: Dean Devlin & Roland Emmerich
Penciled by: Terry Pallot, Steve Erwin, Rod Whigham & Gabriel Gecko
Inked by: Terry Pallot, Phil Moy, Larry Welch & Steve Moncuse
Lettered by: Edd Fear
Colored by: Moose Baumann
Original Series Edits by: Mark Paniccia & Dan Shaheen, with Mark Robert Bourne

INDEPENDENCE DAY #1 & 2

Adapted by: Ralph Macchico
From the Screenplay by: Dean Devlin & Roland Emmerich
Artwork by: Leonard Kirk, Rod Whigham, Terry Pallot, Scott Reed, Steve Erwin & Steve Moncuse
Lettered by: Edd Fear
Colored by: Moose Baumann
Original Series Edits by: Phil Crain, with Mark Robert Bourne

Special Thanks to: Keith Conroy, Leonard Kirk, Cindy Irwin, Jennifer Sebree,
Dionne McNeff, Dean Devlin, Debbie Olshan, Scott Bernstein, Marc Daellenbach,
Steven Fahey, Stan "Fanatic" Froanic & Mike "Geriatric" Giles

JULY 4TH, 1947.

THE STREETS OF THE SMALL DESERT TOWN OF ROSWELL, NEW MEXICO ARE EMPTY. ON THIS NIGHT, THE TOWNSPEOPLE HAVE TAKEN SHELTER IN THEIR HOMES AND LEFT THE CELEBRATING OF THE ANNIVERSARY OF THEIR NATION'S INDEPENDENCE TO MOTHER NATURE.

TONIGHT, SOMETHING HAS VENTURED INTO THE EYE OF THE STORM...

...SOMETHING NOT OF THIS WORLD!

SHRAKKK!

INDEPENDENCE DAY

DR. ROSE FEELS HIS MIND BEING PROBED.

WITH EACH PASSING SECOND, THE PAIN GROWS MORE INTENSE.

GET OUT... AAAAHHH!

A SINGLE WORD IS REPEATED OVER AND OVER AS THE FIRE IN HIS BRAIN SPREADS...

...AND THEN THE LINK IS BROKEN BY DEATH.

DR. ROSE, ARE YOU OKAY? *WHAT* HAPPENED?

YEAH... I DON'T KNOW WHAT HAPPENED.

HE LIES BECAUSE HE'S AFRAID OF THE TRUTH.

THE ALIEN ENTERED HIS MIND. IT REPEATED ONE WORD OVER AND OVER. HE CAN STILL HEAR IT ECHOING IN HIS HEAD.

IT SAID...

'...KILL.'

AND THAT THOUGHT CHILLS DR. ROSE TO THE BONE BECAUSE HE HAS A FEELING THIS IS ONLY THE BEGINNING...

END OF CHAPTER ONE

1986.

FOR RUSSELL CASSE, FLYING IS LIFE'S GREATEST PLEASURE.

ON THIS DAY, HE IS RETURNING HOME AFTER DUSTING A NEARBY CORN FIELD.

THE SKY GROWS DARK...

...BUT THERE ARE NO CLOUDS IN THE SKY.

HIS BIPLANE DIVES HARD...

...THE HUGE CRAFT IS INESCAPABLE.

HE TRIES TO SCREAM, BUT HE'S TOO TERRIFIED.

OH MY GOD.

THEN A BRILLIANT LIGHT SWALLOWS HIM WHOLE.

SILENCE...

RUSSELL AWAKENS TO STRANGE SURROUNDINGS.

HE DOESN'T RECOGNIZE ANYTHING. THE WRITING. THE ARCHITECTURE. NOTHING.

THEN HIS WHOLE BODY FALLS COLD AS HE REALIZES WHERE HE IS...

HE'S ABOARD AN ALIEN SHIP!

AND THERE'S NO ESCAPE!

NO! DON'T TOUCH ME!

A HUMMING SOUND FOCUSES RUSSELL'S WAVERING CONSCIOUSNESS TO HIS LEFT SIDE AND REVEALS ONE OF HIS CAPTORS.

HIS HEART BEGINS TO RACE AS ITS DARK FIGURE SLITHERS CLOSER...

WHAT IS THAT THING?

THE HUMMING GROWS LOUDER AS THE DEVICE IS POISED, HANGING THREATENINGLY CLOSE TO HIS QUIVERING BODY.

THIS CAN'T BE HAPPENING. IT CAN'T BE. NO...

PLEASE STOP. PLEASE DON'T...

PLEASE STOP.

WHY ARE YOU DOING THIS? WHAT DO YOU WANT FROM ME?

TO DIE.

HE TRIES TO RESPOND TO THE ALIEN VOICE INSIDE HIS HEAD...

...BUT THERE IS A SHARP PAIN AND EVERYTHING TURNS TO BLACK...

HOURS LATER...

RUSSELL FINDS HIMSELF IN A STRANGE FIELD AND WITH HOURS OF TIME WHICH ARE UNACCOUNTED FOR.

AS MUCH AS HE TRIES TO TELL HIMSELF HE WASN'T ABDUCTED, HE KNOWS HE IS LYING TO HIMSELF.

HE REMEMBERS EVERYTHING AND HE KNOWS HIS WIFE IS GOING TO THINK HE'S CRAZY.

MARIA'S NOT GOING TO BELIEVE THIS.

MUCH LATER THAT DAY, THOMAS J. WHITMORE AND CONSTANCE SPANO, NOW HIS DIRECTOR OF COMMUNICATIONS, GO OVER THE SEEMINGLY ENDLESS LIST OF APPOINTMENTS.

SECRETARY OF DEFENSE...

DON'T YOU *THINK* WE SHOULD APPOINT SOMEONE INVOLVED WITH THE CAMPAIGN TO THAT OFFICE?

I REALLY WISH I COULD DO THAT, BUT I JUST DON'T THINK ANYBODY ON OUR TEAM HAS ENOUGH EXPERIENCE.

I'VE COME UP WITH ALBERT NIMZIKI. HE'S BEEN IN THE GOVERNMENT SINCE THE SIXTIES. HE'S HELD *SEVERAL* HIGH-RANKING POSITIONS. I THINK HE'S PERFECT.

NIMZIKI! I DON'T THINK THAT'S A WISE CHOICE, TOM.

I MEAN, THE GUY'S WASHINGTON'S *ULTIMATE* INSIDER. ALL HIS MOVES ARE POWER PLAYS.

I DON'T THINK WE CAN TRUST HIM!

I KNOW THIS HAS BEEN A LONG DAY, CONNIE.

WE'RE BOTH TIRED.

I'M SORRY, CONNIE, BUT I'M GOING WITH NIMZIKI.

NOW LET'S MOVE ON.

WHAT'S NEXT?

SECRETARY OF COMMERCE.

THE WHITE HOUSE.

SPIRITS ARE LOW IN THE WHITMORE ADMINISTRATION. IT'S AN ELECTION YEAR AND THE PRESIDENT'S APPROVAL RATING HAS HIT ROCK BOTTOM.

WITH THE ELECTION NEARING, PRESIDENT WHITMORE'S RE-ELECTION SEEMS UNLIKELY.

MANY INSIDERS CHARGE THAT HE CAN'T HANDLE THE POSITION.

THEY SEE HIM AS FAR TOO *PRAGMATIC* A LEADER TO REMAIN IN OFFICE.

EVEN AN UNDISCLOSED MEMBER OF WHITMORE'S CABINET SAID THAT HE WAS "*INDECISIVE* AND *INEFFECTIVE*."

TURN THAT DAMN THING OFF!

WHY? MAYBE WE SHOULD LISTEN TO WHAT THEY HAVE TO SAY.

WHAT? IF I DIDN'T KNOW BETTER, I'D SAY THAT REPORTER WAS QUOTING YOU, ALBERT!

YOU'RE A *SNAKE* IN AN EXPENSIVE SUIT!

THAT'S RIDICULOUS, GENERAL. I'VE--

GENTLE-MEN! LET'S GET A HOLD OF OUR-SELVES.

THAT WAS DECISIVE, WOULDN'T YOU SAY, CONNIE?

DEFINITELY, SIR.

OKUN'S ASSISTANT DROPS LIFELESSLY TO THE FLOOR AS OKUN FLEES IN TERROR.

WHUMP!

EACH STEP HE TAKES SEEMS TO BE IN SLOW MOTION AS THE CREATURE APPROACHES.

HE MAKES IT INTO THE HALLWAY AS A MP COMES UP BEHIND HIM.

GET DOWN, DR. OKUN!

OKUN IS PUSHED ASIDE AS THE MP OPENS FIRE...

...IN VAIN.

NO--!

IN THE INSTANT BEFORE THE MP'S DEATH, OKUN HEARS THE ALIEN'S THOUGHT: 'KILL.'

OKUN FREEZES.

HE STARES UP INTO THE ALIEN'S BLACK EYES AND SEES...

...DEATH.

NO!!

OKUN'S HEART RACES AND HIS MIND CLEARS AS HE REALIZES...

...IT WAS ALL A DREAM-- A NIGHTMARE.

IT'S CLOSE TO MIDNIGHT AND THE LAB'S EMPTY. BUT HE CAN FEEL THE WEIGHT OF THEIR DEAD STARE ON HIS BACK.

SLOWLY HE TURNS, LIKE A SCARED CHILD.

ONE WHO NEEDS TO STARE DOWN THE MONSTER TO MAKE IT GO AWAY.

BUT IT DOESN'T DISAPPEAR.

IT JUST STARES BACK.

OKUN CURSES IT, BECAUSE HE CAN SEE WHAT IT TRULY IS.

HE CAN SEE IT IN ITS DEAD EYES...

...HE CAN SEE EVIL.

JULY 2ND, DOWNTOWN NEW YORK. THE OFFICES OF COMPACT CABLE.

WHAT'S WRONG WITH OUR SIGNAL!? THIS IS A DISASTER!

WHEN MARTY GILBERT WOKE UP THIS MORNING HE KNEW IT WAS GOING TO BE ONE OF THOSE DAYS. HE SAYS THAT EVERY MORNING...

...BUT TODAY HE WAS RIGHT.

HAS ANYBODY SEEN DAVID?

HE'S SCHEDULED TO COME IN AT 10:00, JUST LIKE EVERY DAY, MARTY.

I ALWAYS FORGET THAT.

DOESN'T HE KNOW THIS PLACE GOES TO HELL WHEN HE ISN'T AROUND?

CLIFFSIDE PARK, NEW JERSEY.

YOUR TURN, POP.

SINCE HIS DIVORCE, DAVID SPENDS MOST OF HIS MORNINGS IN THE PARK PLAYING CHESS WITH HIS FATHER, JULIUS. HE LOVES THE CHALLENGE AND IT'S ALWAYS GREAT TO SPEND TIME WITH HIS FATHER.

BEEP! BEEP! BEEP!

HOLD YOUR HORSES! YOU'RE TRYING TO MAKE ME HURRY SO I WILL LOSE!

AREN'T YOU GOING TO ANSWER YOUR PAGE?

NAH. IF IT IS IMPORTANT THEY CAN PAGE ME AGAIN.

IT'S NOT LIKE IT'S THE END OF THE WORLD OR ANYTHING.

THOUSANDS OF MILES
ABOVE THE EARTH,
THERE IS STILLNESS.

BUT TODAY, THAT IS
GOING TO CHANGE.

A DARK SHADOW FALLS
ON THE MOON'S SURFACE...

...AND ENVELOPS IT IN DARKNESS.

THEN THE TRUE
PRIZE IS SEEN...

...EARTH!

49 YEARS AGO, THEY VISITED US DUE TO A NAVIGATIONAL MISHAP.

THAT WAS IN 1947, IN ROSWELL, NEW MEXICO.

NOW THEY'RE BACK AND THEY WANT TO ANNIHILATE.

THE BATTLE BEGINS IN INDEPENDENCE DAY #1. BASED ON THE MOVIE EVENT OF THE SUMMER!

THE EARTH'S MOON BEARS SILENT WITNESS TO THE RELICS OF MANKIND'S EXPLORATION OF HER CRAGGY SURFACE.

BUT, THIS LUNAR DAY, SOMETHING ELSE HAS COME TO THE EONS-OLD SATELLITE....

...SOMETHING OF SUCH POWER THAT ITS VERY APPROACH CAUSES THE REMNANTS OF APOLLO SPACE MISSIONS TO RATTLE AND SHAKE.

THEN, THE MONSTROUS SHADOW OF AN UNFATHOMABLY LARGE CRAFT APPEARS, BLOTTING OUT THE SUN'S RAYS.

AND FOR THE DENIZENS OF THE BLUE-GREEN PLANET SOME TWO HUNDRED AND FIFTY THOUSAND MILES AWAY...

...AN UNIMAGINABLE STRUGGLE FOR THE VERY SURVIVAL OF THEIR WORLD IS ABOUT TO COMMENCE.

INDEPENDENCE

DAY

Script: Ralph Macchio
adapted from the screenplay
by Dean Devlin & Roland Emmerich
Artist: Leonard Kirk
Letterer: edd fear
Colorist: Moose Baumann
Editor: Phil Crain
Editorial Assistant: Mark Robert Bourne
Special thanks to: Cindy Irwin, Jennifer Sebree,
Dionne McNeff, Dean Devlin, Debbie Olshan,
Brian Ferrari, Andy Walton,
& Jennifer Schellinger.

NEW MEXICO. RADIO TELESCOPE VALLEY, WHERE A FIELD OF LARGE TELESCOPE DISHES SCAN THE SKIES FOR SIGNS OF EXTRATERRESTRIAL EXISTENCE.

THE MONITORING CONTROL CENTER OF THE S.E.T.I. INSTITUTE...

SORRY FOR WAKING YOU SIR, BUT I THINK THIS IS THE ONE.

I HOPE IT'S NOT JUST *ANOTHER* RUSSIAN SPY JOB.

NEGATIVE. COMPUTER CONFIRMS THE SIGNAL IS UNIDENTIFIED.

THE BOYS FROM AIR RES TRAFFIC SAY THE SKIES ARE CLEAR. NO TERRESTRIAL LAUNCHES.

BEING DONE.

CALCULATED DISTANCE FROM SOURCE IS AT THREE-HUNDRED AND EIGHTY-FIVE THOUSAND KILOMETERS.

IT'S THE *REAL THING.* A RADIO SIGNAL FROM ANOTHER WORLD.

LET'S NOT JUMP THE GUN. RUN A TRAJECTORY SOURCE COM-PUTATION.

WHERE'S IT COMING FROM?

NO WAY. THIS RADIO SIGNAL'S COMING FROM...

...THE MOON.

THE WHITE HOUSE, CURRENTLY OCCUPIED BY PRESIDENT THOMAS J. WHITMORE...

RING!

HI. IT'S ME.

HI HONEY. WHAT TIME IS IT IN L.A?

TWO IN THE MORNING. I *KNOW* I DIDN'T WAKE YOU.

LIAR.

AS A MATTER OF FACT YOU DID.

ACTUALLY, I HAVE A *CONFESSION* TO MAKE. THERE'S A *BEAUTIFUL* YOUNG BRUNETTE SLEEPING NEXT TO ME.

YOU *DIDN'T* LET HER STAY UP WATCHING T.V. ALL NIGHT?

OF COURSE NOT. PATRICIA, IT'S MOMMY.

THANKS DADDY.

LET'S SEE HOW I'M BEING *SKEWERED* ON THE TUBE.

KLIK

IT'S NOT THAT I HAVE ANYTHING *PERSONAL* AGAINST PRESIDENT WHITMORE BUT--

-- THE INEXPERIENCE IN PUBLIC OFFICE WAS INEVITABLY GOING TO CATCH UP WITH HIM.

HE'S SACRIFICED HIS *IDEALS* FOR "POLITICS AS USUAL."

IN SPACE, AN IMPOSSIBLY LARGE SPACECRAFT HAS POSITIONED ITSELF ABOVE THE EARTH'S ATMOSPHERE.

DOZENS OF SMALLER VESSELS, EACH 15 MILES WIDE THEMSELVES, DISENGAGE FROM THE UNDERBELLY OF THE MOTHERSHIP--

--SPREADING OUT STRATEGICALLY AS THEY BEGIN THEIR OMINOUS JOURNEY TOWARD THE BRIGHT PLANET BELOW.

LIKE HARBINGERS OF THE ARMAGEDDON, THE SPHERICAL CRAFTS DESCEND...

...THEIR TIME OF CONCEALMENT AT AN END...

THE CASSE MOBILE HOME...

WHAT'S THAT *NOISE?* DO YOU SEE ANYTHING?

LOOK, MIGUEL--OVER THE HILLS!

SO *BRIGHT--* AND I CAN FEEL THE *HEAT* FROM HERE! WHAT'S HAPPENING?

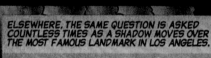

ELSEWHERE, THE SAME QUESTION IS ASKED COUNTLESS TIMES AS A SHADOW MOVES OVER THE MOST FAMOUS LANDMARK IN LOS ANGELES.

LYWOOD

CONNIE--THANK YOU FOR SEEING US. IF I DIDN'T BELIEVE I HAD THE ANSWER TO THE CRISIS, I WOULDN'T BE HERE.

YOU ALWAYS THINK YOU HAVE THE ANSWERS, DAVID.

BUT YOU'VE COME THIS FAR, SO SHOW ME WHAT YOU'VE GOT.

WHITMORE MUST SEE THIS. IT'S THE BREAKDOWN OF THE ALIEN SIGNAL--

--AND THAT PINPOINTS THEIR ATTACK TIME.

LAST TIME I SAW THE PRESIDENT, I *PUNCHED* HIM--

--'CAUSE I THOUGHT HE WAS MAKING A PLAY FOR YOU.

YEAH, BUT HE *WASN'T* PRESIDENT THEN. JUST A SENATOR.

PUNCHED A *PRESIDENT?* OH MY GOD!

I DON'T KNOW HOW WELL YOU'RE GOING TO BE RECEIVED, BUT HERE GOES.

WE DON'T HAVE TIME TO WASTE. GET ME IN THERE.

RIGHT DOWN THIS HALLWAY, PRESIDENT WHITMORE, WE'LL BE ENTERING OUR MAIN MEDICAL LAB.

THE ALIEN WHICH WAS RETRIEVED BY CAPTAIN HILLER WAS BROUGHT DOWN HERE FOR EXAMINATION BY DR. OKUN.

FUNNY... THE GLASS DOORS ARE ALL *STEAMED UP!* I WONDER WHAT'S GOING ON?

RELEASE... ME.

THOMP

OPEN THE DOOR. GET HIM OUT OF THERE.

WAIT!

THAMP

WILL KILL... RELEASE NOW!

WHY DID YOU COME HERE?

AIR... WATER...YOUR "SUN."

WHERE IS YOUR HOME?

BEFORE... MANY WORLDS. NOW...HERE.

CAN WE NEGOTIATE A TRUCE? CAN THERE BE *PEACE* BETWEEN US?

PEACE? NO PEACE.

WHAT DO YOU WANT US TO DO?

DIE.

MAN, I'VE WAITED A LONG TIME FOR THIS...LOOK AT THOSE STARS!

I *SEE* IT! THE MOTHER-SHIP!

THAT *JARRING* SENSATION! SOMETHING'S HAPPENING TO THE CONTROLS-- THEY'RE NOT RESPONDING!

LET ME CHECK MY LAPTOP.

GREAT! I WAS *COUNTING* ON THIS! THEY'VE LOCKED A *TRACTOR BEAM* ON US AND THEY'RE BRINGING US ONBOARD!

THAT'S WHY THE SIGNAL'S CHANGED.

INTO THE *BELLY* OF THE BEAST. HOLD ON!

DEEP INSIDE, DAVID AND STEVEN'S ATTACKER IS GUIDED TO THE DOCKING STATION.

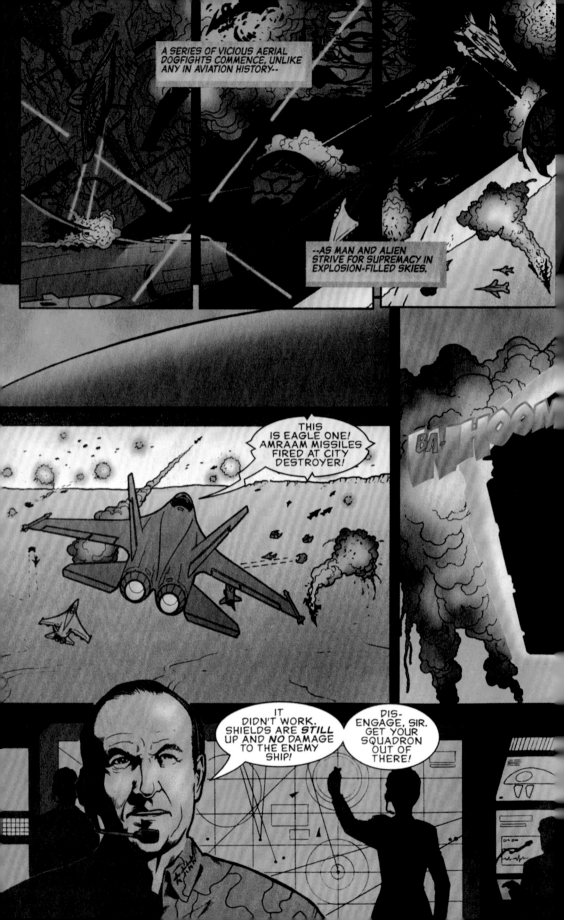

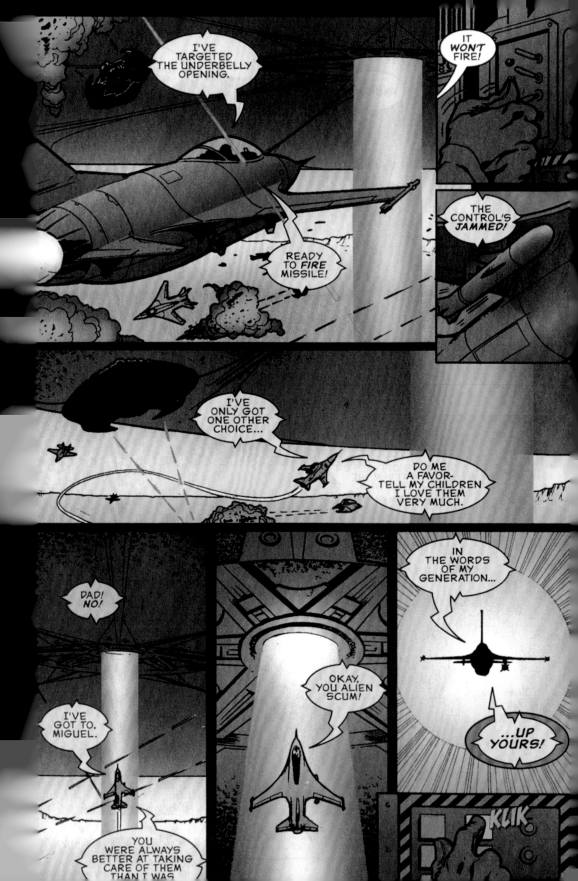

THE ORIGINAL MOVIE ADAPTATION

INDEPENDENCE DAY
RESURGENCE

First Contact
1947 – Roswell, New Mexico
An extraterrestrial craft crashlands near a ranch in Roswell, New Mexico. The US military launches an investigation.

World Mourns Col. Steven Hiller
2007 (Area 51, Nevada) – 4/27/07
While test piloting the ESD's first alien hybrid fighter, an unknown malfunction causes the untimely death of Col. Hiller. He is survived by his wife Jasmine and son Dylann.

The World Rebuilds
1997 (London, UK) – 11/30/97
The alien threat has been all but neutralized – and the world begins to rise from the ashes. Reconstruction starts immediately as the great cities, monuments and landmarks of the world are slowly restored to their former glory.

Silent Zone
1970s (Nevada Desert)
Dr. Brackish Okun arrives at Area 51 to work with the NSA and CIA on the study of the New Mexico ship.

Arrival & Attack
1996 (Middle of Atlantic) – 7/2/96
A massive alien mothership enters Earth's orbit, deploying 36 City Destroyers to annihilate the world's largest cities. Within 48 hours, 108 cities are reduced to ashes.

Earth Strikes Back
1996 (Nevada Desert) 7/4/96
Earth's nations launch a globally coordinated counterattack, destroying the alien mothership and eliminating the extraterrestrial threat.

Honoring 20 Years of Global Unity
2016 (Washington D.C.) – 7/4/16
As we remember the last 20 years, we must also look to the future. The world has rebuilt stronger then we ever imagined and we must promise ourselves, as well as future generations, that we're never caught off guard again. We must continue to work together to secure the future of the human race – for as long as we stay united, we will survive.

U.S. Army Adopts Alien Weaponry 2004 (El Paso, Texas) – 10/23/03
Applying new data from recovered alien weaponry, U.S. Army scientists make dramatic advances in applying their findings to military applications.

Terror From The Deep
1996 (Atlantic Ocean) 7/5/96
A functioning extraterrestrial craft is discovered beneath the Atlantic Ocean. An investigation – headed by Captain Adams – is implemented by the US military.

WELCOME TO EARTH

SILENT ZONE
INDEPENDENCE DAY

INDEPENDENCE DAY

TAKE THE TECH

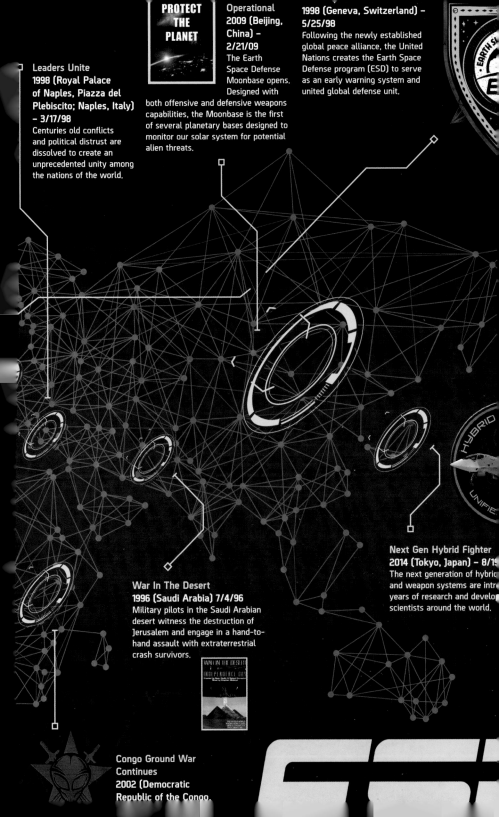

PROTECT THE PLANET

Leaders Unite
1998 (Royal Palace of Naples, Piazza del Plebiscito; Naples, Italy) – 3/17/98
Centuries old conflicts and political distrust are dissolved to create an unprecedented unity among the nations of the world.

Operational 2009 (Beijing, China) – 2/21/09
The Earth Space Defense Moonbase opens. Designed with both offensive and defensive weapons capabilities, the Moonbase is the first of several planetary bases designed to monitor our solar system for potential alien threats.

1998 (Geneva, Switzerland) – 5/25/98
Following the newly established global peace alliance, the United Nations creates the Earth Space Defense program (ESD) to serve as an early warning system and united global defense unit.

War In The Desert
1996 (Saudi Arabia) 7/4/96
Military pilots in the Saudi Arabian desert witness the destruction of Jerusalem and engage in a hand-to-hand assault with extraterrestrial crash survivors.

Next Gen Hybrid Fighter
2014 (Tokyo, Japan) – 8/19
The next generation of hybrid and weapon systems are intr... years of research and develop... scientists around the world.

Congo Ground War Continues
2002 (Democratic Republic of the Congo,

INDEPENDENCE DAY

VICTOR GISCHLER   STEVE SCOTT